Enid Blyton

A FARAWAY TREE

Adventure

The Land of
DO-AS-YOU-PLEASE

For Wilby and Lottie
A. P.

EGMONT
We bring stories to life

Cover and interior illustrations by Alex Paterson

Text first published in Great Britain as chapters 11-12
of *The Magic Faraway Tree* 1943
Published as *The Land of Do-As-You-Please: A Faraway Tree Adventure* 2016
by Egmont UK Limited
The Yellow Building, 1 Nicholas Road, London W11 4AN

Text copyright © 1943 Hodder & Stoughton Ltd.
ENID BLYTON ® Copyright © 2016 Hodder & Stoughton Ltd.
ENID BLYTON ® Illustrations Copyright © 2016 Hodder & Stoughton Ltd.

ISBN 978 1 4052 8009 9

www.egmont.co.uk

A CIP catalogue record for this title is available from the British Library

Printed in Malaysia

62078/1

MIX
Paper
FSC   FSC® C018306

Enid Blyton

A FARAWAY TREE

Adventure

The Land of
DO-AS-YOU-PLEASE

EGMONT

The World of the FARAWAY TREE

MOON-FACE lives at the very top. In his house is the start of the **SLIPPERY-SLIP**, a huge slide that curves all the way down inside the trunk of the tree.

SILKY lives below Moon-Face. She is the prettiest little fairy you ever did see.

SAUCEPAN MAN is a funny old thing. His saucepans make lots of noise when they jangle together, so he can't hear very well.

CHAPTER ONE
A Message from Silky and Moon-Face

The children hadn't visited the Enchanted Wood for a whole week. For one thing they were **very busy helping their parents,** and for another thing they felt that they didn't want any adventures for a little while.

1

And then a note came from Silky and Moon-Face. This is what it said:

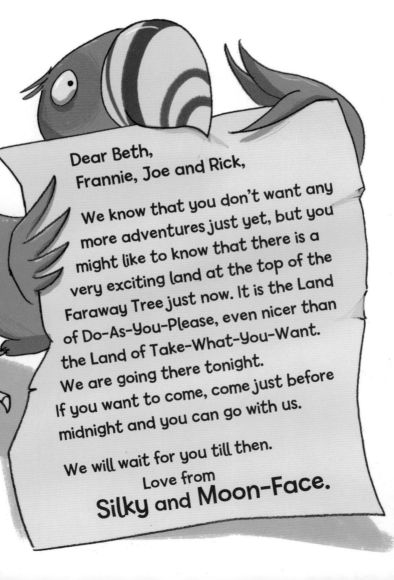

Dear Beth,
Frannie, Joe and Rick,

We know that you don't want any more adventures just yet, but you might like to know that there is a very exciting land at the top of the Faraway Tree just now. It is the Land of Do-As-You-Please, even nicer than the Land of Take-What-You-Want. We are going there tonight. If you want to come, come just before midnight and you can go with us.

We will wait for you till then.
Love from
Silky and Moon-Face.

The children read the note one after another. **Their eyes began to shine. 'Shall we go?'** said Frannie.

'Better not,' said Joe. 'Something silly is sure to happen to us. It always does.'

'Oh, Joe! Do let's go!' said Beth. 'You know how exciting the Enchanted Wood is at night, too, with all the fairy-folk about – and the Faraway Tree lit with lanterns and things. Come on, Joe – say we'll go.'

'I really think we'd better not,' said Joe. 'Rick might do something silly again.'

'I would **not!**' said Rick in a temper. 'It's not fair of you to say that.'

'Don't quarrel,' said Beth. 'Well, listen — if you don't want to go, Joe, **Frannie and I will go with Rick.** He can look after us.'

'**Pooh!** Rick wants looking after himself,' said Joe. Rick pulled a face at Joe, and Joe pulled a face back.

'**Oh, don't!**' said Beth. 'You're not in the Land of Do-As-You-Please now!' That made everyone laugh.

'Sorry, Joe,' said Rick. **'Be a sport. Let's all go tonight.** Or at any rate, let's go up the tree and hear what Silky and Moon-Face can tell us about this new land. If it sounds at all dangerous we won't go. OK?'

'All right,' said Joe, who really did want to go just as badly as the others, but felt that he shouldn't keep leading them into danger. 'All right. We'll go up and talk to Silky and Moon-Face. But remember – if I decide not to go with them, there's to be no grumbling.'

'We promise, Joe,' said Beth.

And so it was settled. They would go to the Enchanted Wood that night and climb the Faraway Tree to see their friends.

CHAPTER TWO
Off to the Enchanted Wood

It was exciting to slip out of bed at half past eleven and dress. It was very dark because there was no moon.

'We shall have to take a pocket light,' said Joe. **'Are you all ready?** Now don't make a noise, or you'll wake Mother and Father.'

They all **crept downstairs** and out into the dark, silent garden.

An owl **hooted** nearby, and
something ran down the garden path.
Beth nearly squealed.

'**Shh!** It's only a mouse or something,' said Joe. 'I'll switch on my light now. **Keep close together and we'll see where we're going.**'

In a bunch they went down the back garden and out into the little lane there. The Enchanted Wood loomed up big and dark. The trees spoke to one another softly.

'**wisha-wisha-wisha,**' they said. '**Wisha-wisha-wisha!**'

The children jumped over the ditch and walked through the wood, down the paths they knew so well. **The wood was full of fairy-folk going about their business.**

They took no notice of the children.

Joe soon switched off his light.

Lanterns shone everywhere and

gave enough light to see by.

They soon came to the great dark trunk
of the Faraway Tree. A rope swung down
through the branches.

'**Oh, good!**' said Rick. 'Is Moon-Face
going to pull us up?'

'No,' said Joe. 'We'll have to climb up –
but we can use the rope to help us.
It's always in the tree at night to help the
many folk going up and down.'

And indeed there were a great many
people using the Faraway Tree that night.
Strange pixies, goblins and gnomes
swarmed up and down it, and elves
climbed up, chattering hard.

15

'Where are they going?' asked Rick in surprise.

'Oh, up to the Land of Do-As-You-Please, I expect,' said Joe. 'And some of them are visiting their friends in the tree. **Look, there's the Angry Pixie!** He's got a party on tonight!'

The Angry Pixie had about eight little friends squashed into his tree-room, and looked as pleased as could be.

'Come and join us!' he called to Joe.

'We can't,' said Joe. 'Thanks all the same. We're going up to Moon-Face's.'

16

Everyone dodged Dame
Washalot's washing water, laughed
at old Watzisname sitting snoring
as usual in his chair, and at last
came to Moon-Face's house.

And there was nobody there!
**There was a note stuck on
the door.**

'Gosh!' said Rick, longingly. 'What I'd like to do better than anything else is to ride six times on a roundabout without stopping!'

'And I'd like to eat six ice-creams **without stopping!**' said Beth.

'And I'd like to ride an **elephant,**' said Frannie.
'And I would like to drive a train **all by myself,**' said Joe.

'Joe! *Let's* go up the ladder!' said Beth. 'Oh, please, please let's go!

'Why can't we go and visit a really nice land when one comes?' begged Frannie. 'It's so mean of you to say we can't.'

'Well,' said Joe. **'I suppose we'd better! Come on!'**

CHAPTER THREE
The Land of Do-As-You-Please

With shrieks of delight the girls and Rick raced up the ladder, through the cloud. A lantern hung at the top of the hole to give them light – **but, lo and behold,** as soon as they had got into the land above the cloud it was daytime!

How magical!

23

The children stood and gazed round it.
It seemed a very exciting land, rather like
a huge amusement park.

There were roundabouts going round
and round in time to music. There were
swings and see-saws.

There was a train **puffing along** busily, and there were small planes flying everywhere, with elves, pixies and goblins having a fine time in them.

'Goodness! Doesn't it look exciting?' said Beth. 'I wonder where Moon-Face and Silky are?'

'There they are – **over there** – on that roundabout!' cried Joe. 'Look, Silky is riding a tiger that is going up and down all the time – and Moon-Face is on a giraffe! **Let's get on, too!'**

Off they all ran. As soon as
Moon-Face and Silky saw the children,
they screamed with joy and waved their
hands. The roundabout stopped and the
children got on.

Beth chose a white rabbit. Frannie rode on a lion and **felt very grand.** Joe went on a bear and Rick chose a horse.

'So glad you came!' cried Silky. 'We waited and waited for you. **Oh – we're off! Hold tight!'**

The roundabout went round and round and round. The children shouted excitedly, because it went so fast.

'Let's have six rides without getting off!' cried Joe. So they did – and **whoops,** they *were* giddy when they did at last get off. They rolled about like drunken sailors! **'I feel like sitting down with six ice-creams,'** said Beth.

At once an ice-cream man drove up and handed them out thirty-six ice-creams. **It did look a lot.** When Joe had divided them all out equally there were six each.

And how **delicious** they were!

Everybody managed six quite easily.

'And now, what about me driving that train!' cried Joe, jumping up. 'I've always wanted to do that. Would you all like to be my passengers? Well, come on, then!'

And off they all raced to where the train was stopping at a little station.

'**Hi there!**' yelled Joe to the driver.
'I want to drive your train!'

'Come along up, then,' said the driver,
jumping down. '**It's ready to go!**'

CHAPTER FOUR
Joe the Train Driver

Joe **jumped up** into the engine of the train. A bright fire was burning there, as it was a steam train. He looked at all the shining handles and wheels.

'How shall I know which is which?' he asked the driver.

'Well,' said the driver, pointing to the different knobs and handles. 'That's the **starting wheel** – and that's to make the **whistle** go – and that's to **go slow** – and that's to **go fast.** You can't make a mistake. Don't forget to stop at the stations, will you? And oh – look out for the road crossing gates, in case they are shut. It would be dangerous not to take care there.'

Joe felt tremendously excited.

Rick looked up longingly. 'Joe! Could I come too?' he begged. 'Please let me. Just to watch you.'

'All right,' said Joe. So Rick hopped up on to the engine. Beth, Frannie, Moon-Face and Silky got into a carriage just

behind. The guard ran alongside waving a
flag and blowing his whistle.

'The signal's down!' yelled Rick. 'Go on,
Joe! Start her up!'

Joe twisted the starting wheel. The
engine began to **chuff-chuff-chuff**
and moved out of the station.

'Joe's really driving the train!' cried Beth. **'Oh, isn't he clever!** He's always wanted to drive an engine!'

The engine began to go very fast – too fast. Joe pulled the **'Go Slow'** handle, and it went more slowly. He was so interested in what he was doing that he didn't notice they were coming to a station. **He shot right through it!**

'Joe!' cried Rick. 'You've gone through a station. **Gosh, the passengers waiting there did look cross** – and oh, look, a lot of them in our train wanted to get out there!'

Sure enough, quite a number of angry people were looking out of the carriage windows, yelling to Joe to stop.

Joe went red. He pulled the **'Stop'** handle. The engine stopped.

Then Joe pulled the **'Go Backwards'** handle and the train moved slowly backwards to the station. It stopped there and Joe and Rick had the pleasure of seeing the passengers get out and in.

The guard came rushing up. 'You passed the station, you passed the station!' he cried. 'Don't you dare to pass my station again without stopping!'

'All right, all right,' said Joe. **'Now then – off we go again!'**

And off they went.

'Keep a look-out for stations, signals, tunnels and road crossings, Rick,' said Joe. So Rick stuck his head out and watched.

'Road crossing!' he cried. 'The gates are shut! **Slow down, Joe, slow down!'** But unluckily Joe pulled the '**Go Fast'** handle instead of the '**Go Slow'** and the train shot forward quickly.

Just as the engine reached the gates,
Joe pulled on the brakes.

A little man rushed out of the cabin
nearby, just as the train came to a halt.

'**You bad driver!**' he shouted. 'You might have caused an accident!'

'That was a **narrow escape,**' said Joe.

When the road crossing gates were open, Joe started off again.

'What's coming now, Rick?' Joe asked.

'A tunnel,' said Rick. 'Whistle as you go through in case anyone is working in it.'

So Joe made the engine whistle loudly.

It really was fun. It raced through the dark tunnel and came out near a station.

'Stop! Station, Joe!' cried Rick. And Joe stopped. Then on went the train again, whistling loudly, rushing past signals that were down. Then something happened. The **'Go Slow'** and the **'Stop'** handles wouldn't work! The train raced on and on past stations, big and small, through tunnels, and past signals that were up.

50

It behaved just as if it had gone mad.

'**Hey!**' said Rick in alarm. '**What's gone wrong, Joe?**'

Joe didn't know. For miles and miles the train tore on, and all the passengers became alarmed.

Then, as the train drew near a station, it gave a **Loud Sigh**, ran slowly and then stopped all by itself.

And it was the very same station it had started from!

CHAPTER FIVE
Elephant Rides

The driver of the train was there, waiting.

'So you're back again,' he said. 'My, you've been quick.'

'Well, the engine didn't behave itself very well,' said Joe, stepping down thankfully. 'It just ran away the last part of the journey. It wouldn't stop anywhere!'

'Oh, I dare say it wanted to get back to me,' said the driver, climbing into the engine. 'It's naughty sometimes. Come along and drive it again with me.'

'**No, thank you,**' said Joe. 'I think I've had enough. It was fun, though.'

Beth, Frannie, Moon-Face and Silky got out of their carriages.

They had been rather frightened the last part of the journey, but they thought Joe was very clever to drive the train by himself.

They all left the station. **'Now what shall we do?'** said Moon-Face.

'I want to ride on an elephant,' said Frannie at once.

'There aren't any,'
said Beth. But no sooner had
she spoken than the children saw **six big grey elephants** walking solemnly up to
them, swaying a little from side to side.

'Oh, look, look!' yelled Frannie,
filled with excitement. **'There are my elephants. Six of them! We can all have a ride!'**

Each elephant had a rope
ladder going up its left side,
leading to a little seat
which was fixed around
the elephant's back.

The children, Moon-Face and Silky each
climbed up the rope ladder and sat on a
comfortable seat on an elephant's back.

Then the big creatures set off, swaying through the crowds. **It was lovely.**

Frannie did enjoy herself. She called to the others. 'Wasn't this a good idea of mine, everybody? Aren't we high up? And isn't it fun?'

'It *is* fun,' said Moon-Face, who had never even seen an elephant before, and would certainly never have thought of riding one if he had.

'Oh, goodness –' he went on. 'My rope ladder has slipped off my elephant! Now I shall never be able to get down! I'll have to ride on this elephant **all my life!**'

Everybody laughed, but Moon-Face was really alarmed. When the children had had enough of riding they all climbed down their rope ladders – but poor Moon-Face sat up on his elephant, looking very worried.

'I tell you I can't get down,' he kept saying. **'I'm up here for good!'**

61

The elephant stood patiently for a little while. Then it swung its **enormous trunk** round, wound it gently round Moon-Face's waist, and lifted him down to the ground. Moon-Face was so surprised that he couldn't speak.

At last he found his tongue. 'What did the elephant lift me down with?' he asked. 'His nose!'

'No, his trunk,' said Joe, laughing. 'Didn't you know that elephants had trunks, Moon-Face?'

'No,' said Moon-Face, puzzled. **'I'm glad he didn't pack me away as baggage!'**

The children laughed. They watched the big elephants walking off.

CHAPTER SIX
To the Sea

'What shall we do now?' said Joe. 'Rick, what do you want to do?'

'Well, I know I can't do it – but I would love to wade in the sea!' said Rick.

'Oooh, that *would* be nice!' said Frannie, who loved wading too. 'But there isn't any sea here.'

Just as she said that she noticed a signpost nearby. It pointed away from them and said, in big letters: **TO THE SEA.**

'Wow, look at that!' said Frannie. 'Come on everyone!' Off they all went, running the way the signpost pointed.

And, after going round two corners, there, sure enough, was the blue sea, lying bright and calm in the warm sunshine! **Shining golden sands stretched to the little waves.**

'Oh, good!' cried Rick, taking off his shoes and socks at once. 'Come on!'

Soon everyone was wading in the warm sea. Moon-Face and Silky had never

waded before, but they loved it just as much as the children did. Rick went out so far that he got his clothes soaking wet.

'Oh Rick! You're wet!' cried Beth. 'Come back!'

'This is the Land of Do-As-You-Please, isn't it?' shouted Rick, jumping about in the water and getting wetter. **'Well, I'll get as wet as I like, then!'**

'Let's make a **HUGE** sandcastle!' cried Moon-Face. 'Then we can all sit on top when the sea comes up.'

'We can't,' said Silky, suddenly looking disappointed.

'Why not?' cried Joe. **'Isn't this the Land of Do-As- You-Please?'**

'Yes,' said Silky. 'But I'm afraid it's time we went back to the Faraway Tree.

This land will soon be on the move – and nice as it is, **we don't want to live here for ever.'**

'Gosh, no,' said Joe. 'Our parents couldn't do without us! **Rick! Come back!** We're going home!'

Rick didn't want to be left behind. He waded back at once, his clothes dripping wet.

They all made their way to the hole
that led down through the cloud to the
Faraway Tree.

'We did have a **lovely** time,' sighed Joe,

looking back longingly at the happy land he was leaving behind. **'It's one of the nicest** lands that has ever been at the top of the tree.'

They all felt tired as they crowded into Moon-Face's room. 'Don't fall asleep before you get home,' said Moon-Face. 'Take cushions, all of you.'

They went down the slippery-slip, yawning. **They made their way home and fell into bed, tired out but happy.**

And in the morning their mother spoke to Rick.

'Rick, why are your clothes so wet this morning?'

'I waded **too deep** in the sea,' said Rick — and he couldn't understand why his Aunt Polly said he was a naughty little story-teller!

The FARAWAY TREE Adventures

Collect them all!

Enid Blyton
A FARAWAY TREE
Adventure
The Land of
BIRTHDAYS

Enid Blyton
A FARAWAY TREE
Adventure
The Land of
MAGIC MEDICINES

Enid Blyton
A FARAWAY TREE
Adventure
The Land of
DO-AS-YOU-PLEASE

Enid Blyton
A FARAWAY TREE
Adventure
The Land of
GOODIES

Each book a classic short story
from the magical Faraway Tree series
with exciting new colour illustrations